Once
There Was a Tree

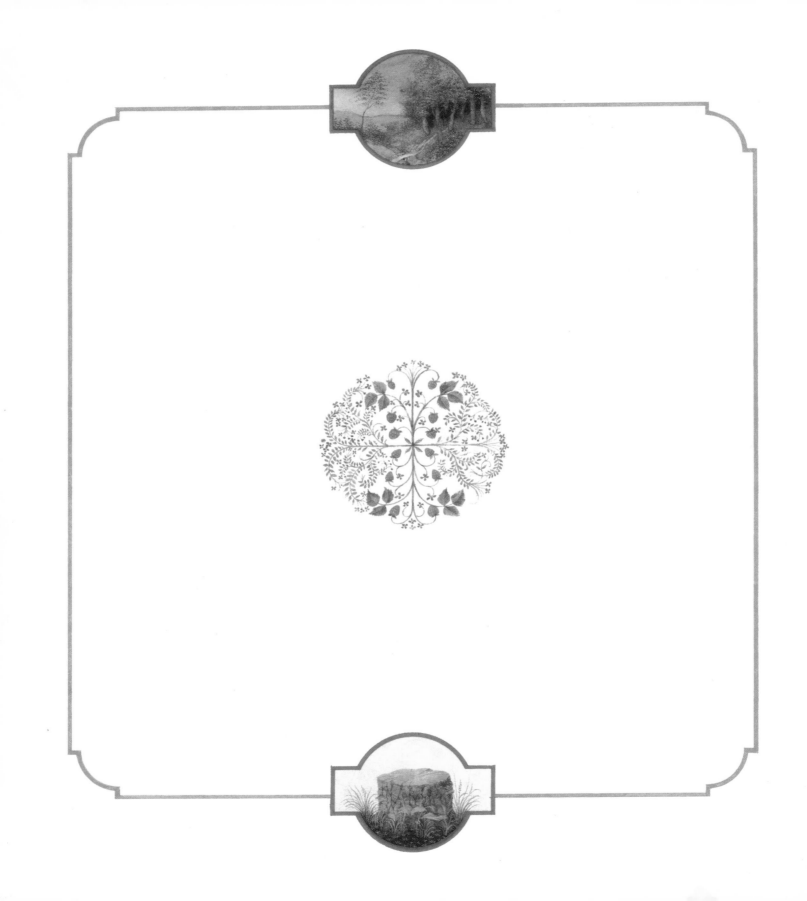

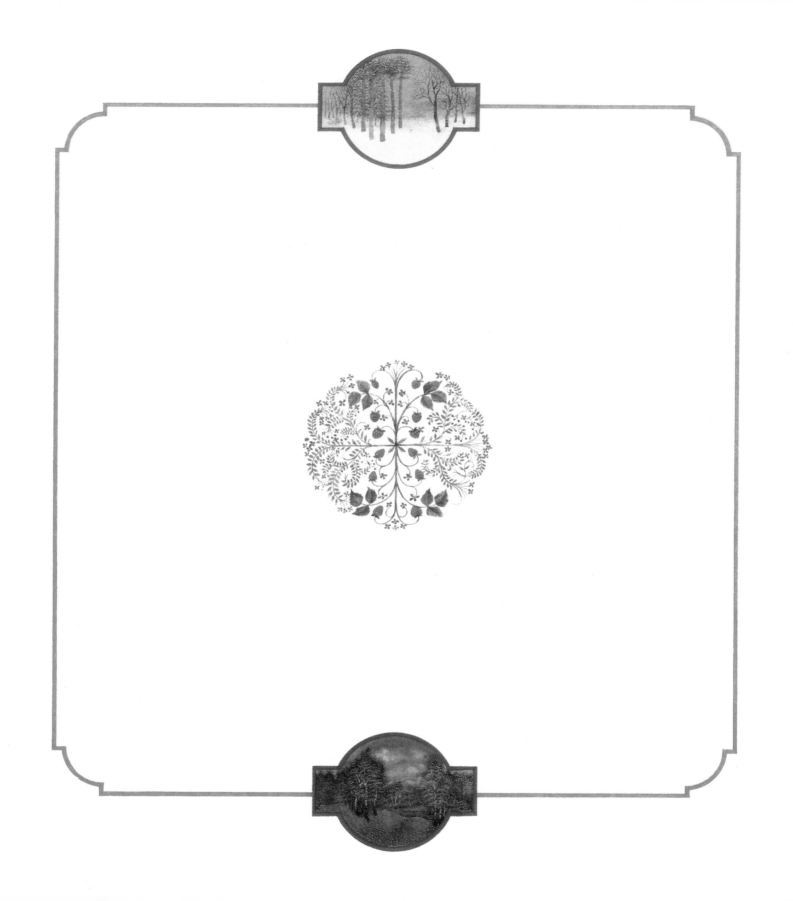

First published in the United States 1985 by
Dial Books
A Division of Penguin Books USA Inc.
2 Park Avenue, New York, New York 10016

Published in Russian in 1983 as *Chei eto pen?*
Copyright © 1983 by Detskaya Literatura, Moscow
Published in German in 1985 as *Unser Baumstumpf*
Copyright © 1985 by K. Thienemanns Verlag, Stuttgart
This translation copyright © 1985 by Dial Books

Adapted by Anne Schwartz

All rights reserved
Library of Congress Catalog Card Number: 85-6730
Printed in Hong Kong by South China Printing Co.
First Pied Piper Printing 1989
D
1 3 5 7 9 10 8 6 4 2

A Pied Piper Book is a registered trademark of
Dial Books, a division of Penguin Books USA Inc.,
®TM 1,163,686 and ®TM 1,054,312.

ONCE THERE WAS A TREE
is published in a hardcover edition by Dial Books.
ISBN 0-8037-0705-3

Once
There Was a Tree

by NATALIA ROMANOVA

pictures by GENNADY SPIRIN

DIAL BOOKS

New York

Once there was a tree. It had grown for many years and now it was growing old.

Dark clouds swept across the sky. Rain fell, thunder
roared, and a lightning   bolt split the tree in two.

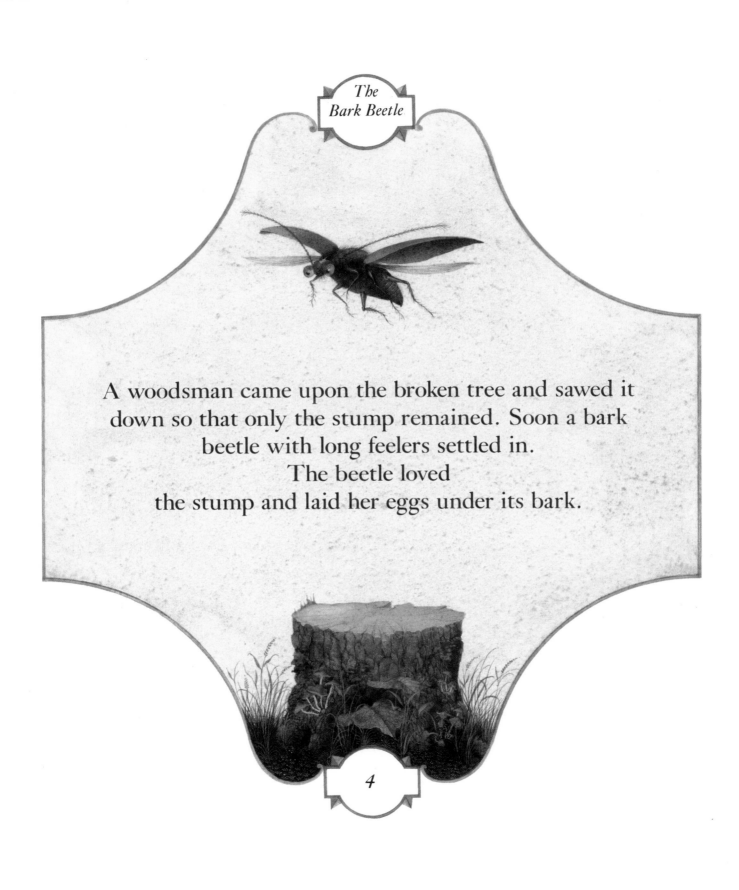

A woodsman came upon the broken tree and sawed it
down so that only the stump remained. Soon a bark
beetle with long feelers settled in.
The beetle loved
the stump and laid her eggs under its bark.

The
Woodsman

5

The eggs hatched and tiny maggots emerged.
All summer long they gnawed tunnels in the bark.
Winter came and they slept. When they
awoke in the spring with long feelers of
their own, it was time to fly away.

But the tree stump was not deserted for long.
With all the entrances and exits the maggots had
made, here was the perfect place for ants
to live. One ant brought a leaf, another a twig,
and another a grain of sand. They cleared out the
tunnels and made the stump their home.

A bear approached the tree stump, sniffed at
it, and sharpened her claws on the bark.
The stump was hers, like everything else around.
Even the ants in the stump were hers, and
no other bear would dare disturb them.

11

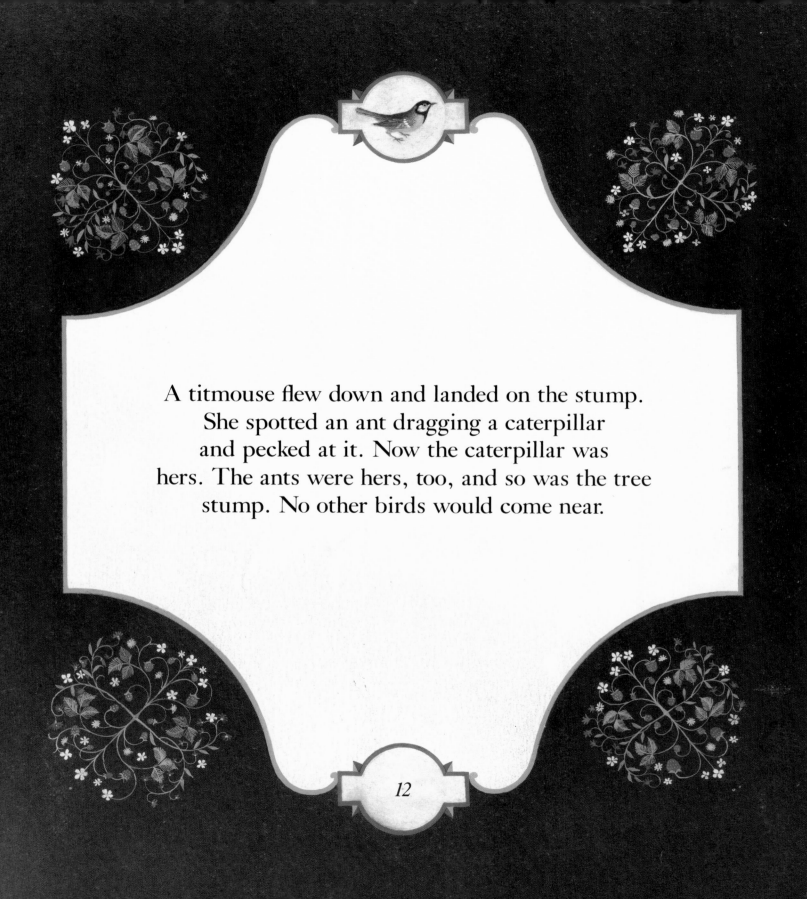

A titmouse flew down and landed on the stump.
She spotted an ant dragging a caterpillar
and pecked at it. Now the caterpillar was
hers. The ants were hers, too, and so was the tree
stump. No other birds would come near.

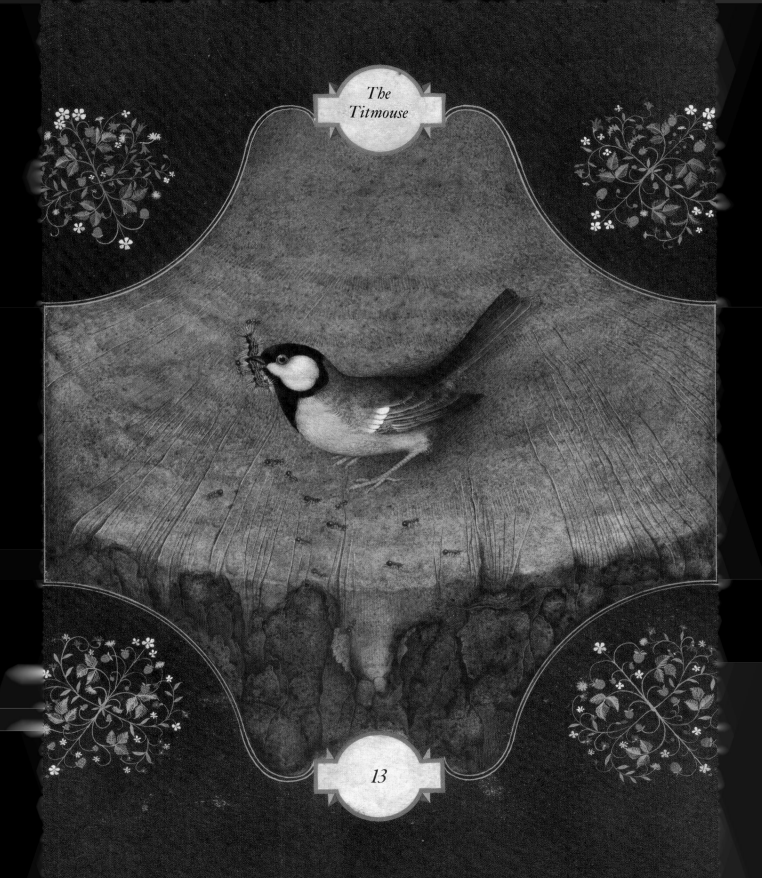

The
Titmouse

13

One rainy day a frog found shelter
in a hole in the tree stump.
Time and weather had dug these holes,
which would protect others who also passed by.

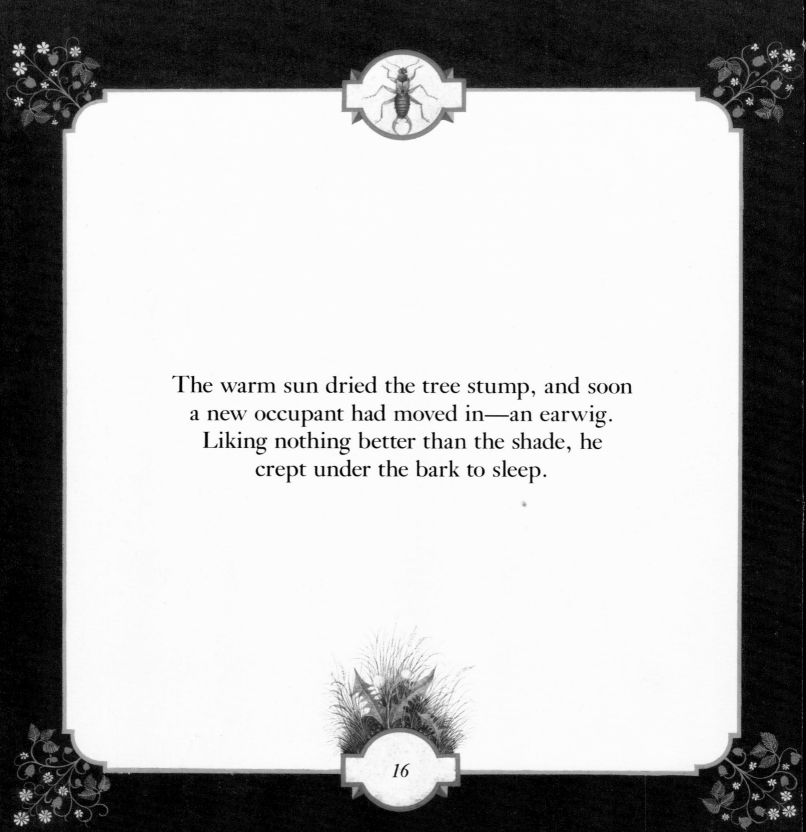

The warm sun dried the tree stump, and soon
a new occupant had moved in—an earwig.
Liking nothing better than the shade, he
crept under the bark to sleep.

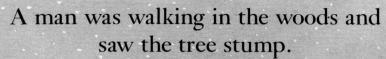

A man was walking in the woods and
saw the tree stump.

He sat down on it to rest, and now the tree stump was his.

The man thought he owned the forest—and the earth—
so why not the tree stump?

But who really owns the tree stump? The bark
beetle that gnaws tunnels inside it?
The ants that travel through the tunnels?
The earwig that sleeps under its bark?
Or the bear that uses it to sharpen her claws?

Does it belong to the titmouse that
flies down upon it? The frog that
finds shelter in one of its holes?
Or the man who believes he
owns the forest?

Maybe the tree stump belongs to all—the
beetle and the ants, the bear and the
titmouse, the frog, the earwig, and even
the man. All must live together.
Meanwhile the tree stump gets older and
older. The sun warms it; the rain cools it.
Soon it begins to rot. Night comes,
and the forest is cast in moonlight.
What remains of the tree stump glows in the dark.

23

Now the tree stump is gone.
A new tree has grown in its place.

A titmouse is perched in its

branches—it is her tree.

An ant  crawls up high—

on her tree.

A bear lumbers by

and sharpens his claws on the bark.
A man lies down to rest in its shade.
The tree belongs to all, because it grows
from the earth that is home for all.

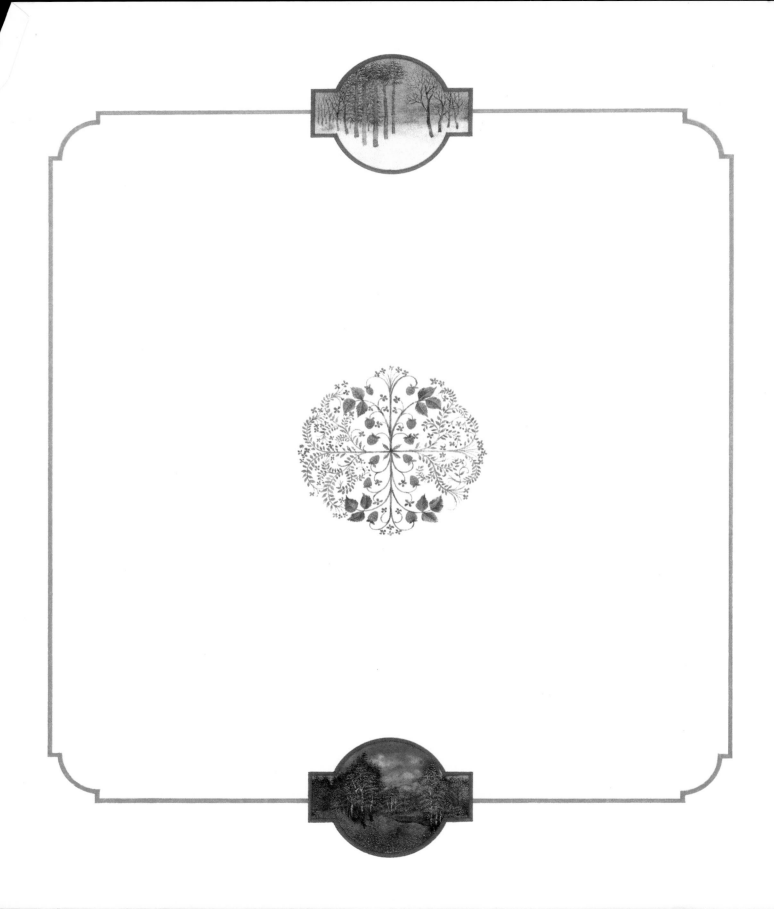

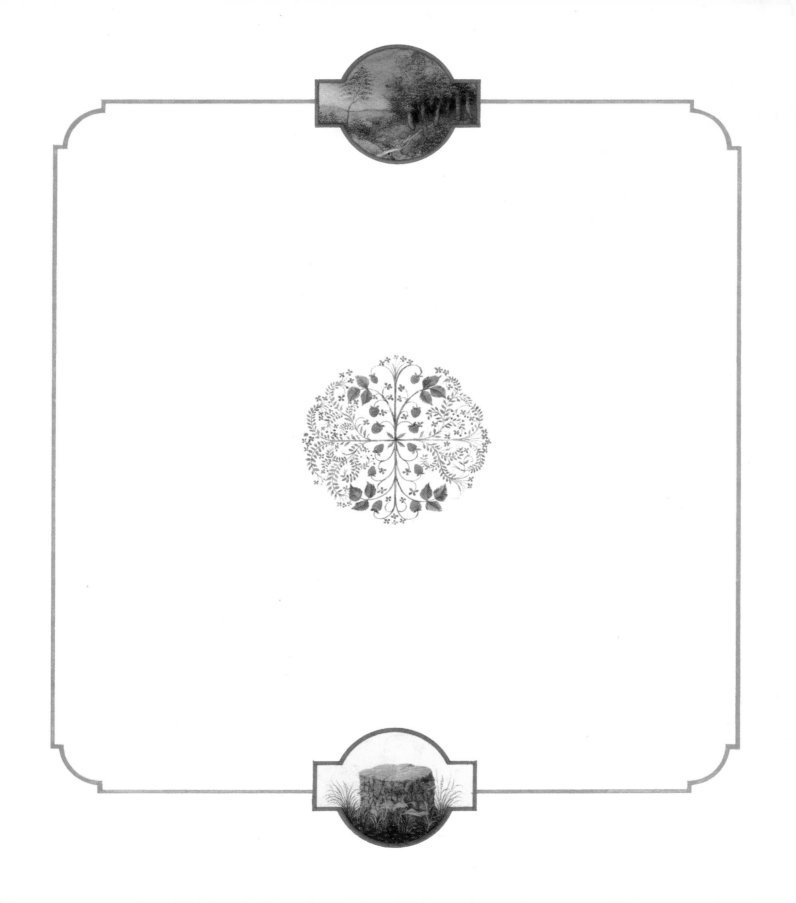